Magical Makeovers

Follow the Glitter Girls' latest adventures!
Collect all the fantastic books in the series:

1 Glitter FM
2 Magical Makeovers
3 Disco Divas
4 Ballet Babes

Caroline Plaisted

Magical Makeovers

SCHOLASTIC

Scholastic Children's Books,
Commonwealth House, 1-19 New Oxford Street,
London WC1A 1NU, UK
a division of Scholastic Ltd

London ~ New York ~ Toronto ~ Sydney ~ Auckland
Mexico City ~ New Delhi ~ Hong Kong

Published by Scholastic Ltd, 2001

ISBN 0 439 99406 3

Typeset by Falcon Oast Graphic Art Ltd
Printed by Cox & Wyman Ltd, Reading, Berks.

6 8 10 9 7 5

Chapter 1

It was Friday afternoon, and Hannah, Flo, Meg, Charly and Zoe – best known to everyone as the Glitter Girls – had just finished school, and were walking towards Zoe's mum's car. Zoe's mum, Dr Baker, was taking them home.

"So, what are we going to do?" asked Meg, tucking a stray piece of her long, wavy blonde hair behind her ear. She was lugging her cello along as well as struggling with her book bag. Friday afternoons were music afternoons at the girls' school and, today, Meg and the other children who played instruments had been asked to bring them along to make up an orchestra.

"Whatever we do, it's got to be great!" said Hannah enthusiastically.

"Course it has! But what are we going to do?" Charly said impatiently.

"Do about what?" Dr Baker asked, opening the back door of her car.

"The school fête. Mrs Wadhurst asked all of us at assembly to think of what stalls we could run at the fête," said Flo, climbing into the car behind Zoe.

"The school fête already?" said Dr Baker in disbelief. "It only seems like yesterday that you girls were running the tombola stall at the last fête."

"Well, the tombola stall is going to be done by some of the boys this year," Meg said, piling into the car behind the others.

"And anyway," muttered Hannah, bending over balletically to pick up her book bag, which she'd dropped, "we've got to do something different, haven't we?"

"But what?" moaned Zoe. "Some of the other girls are doing a craft stall. And Mrs Wilmott is going to run the donkey and pony rides with her daughter and the people from the Donkey Sanctuary."

"I'm sure you'll think of something," smiled Dr Baker, driving away from school. "You Glitter Girls always have great ideas, don't you? So I'm certain you'll be doing something really terrific at the fête."

The journey home wasn't far and the Glitter Girls chatted away about the other stalls that their friends were going to be running. But none of them could think of an idea for something new.

"Right," said Zoe, "I've got to hurry up and get changed for my riding lesson. But I'll see you lot at Charly's house tomorrow morning – we can talk more then."

Hannah grabbed her book bag and jumped down from the car. "I've got to rush too – my mum's taking me to my ballet lesson. See you girls! Thanks Dr Baker!" And she was off down the road to her house.

"Bye!" the others called.

"So we'll meet up at my house tomorrow at nine, then?" Charly said to Flo and Meg.

"You bet! I can't wait to see Girl's Dream," said Flo.

Girl's Dream was a new shop that had opened at the big shopping centre just outside town. The Glitter Girls had read about it in the paper and it sounded fantastic! The article had said that the shop had all sorts of things that girls would love: hair accessories, make-up, clothes, bags, pens and pencils – everything that girls could dream of!

"I'd better rush too – there's my dad!" said Meg. "See you all tomorrow! Bye Dr Baker!"

Meg and her older brother and sister didn't live with their dad and this afternoon he was collecting them from home to take them out to tea.

"Bye Meg!" said Charly and Flo, who were the only two left.

"Come on, let's go. Mum says she's going to let us have pizza for tea!" said Charly.

"My favourite!" said Flo, and she followed Charly to her house, more than happy to eat pizza while she waited for her mum and dad to get home from work.

Chapter 2

The girls were ready promptly the next morning. They couldn't wait to get to Girl's Dream!

Flo and Meg were the first to arrive. As soon as they entered Charly's bedroom they spotted a great new set of hair slides that her aunt who lived in America had sent her.

"This one is just gorgeous!" said Meg, who, like Charly, loved wearing things in her hair. Both girls had long blonde hair, only Charly's was straight and not wavy like Meg's.

Meg picked up the slide. It was lovely – a tiny, pink, fluffy monkey attached to two clips that you pinched together to make it open. Then you wrapped it around some hair to make it grip. The monkey looked like it was hugging your hair!

"Isn't it great?" agreed Charly, pushing her pink glasses back up her nose. "Why don't you try it on?"

"Thanks," said Meg, going over to the mirror.

"I'll help you put it on," Flo said, following her.

Just then, there was a knock at the door.

"Who is it?" asked Charly.

"GG!" whispered voices on the other side.

"GG" was the secret password the Glitter Girls used whenever they got together for a meeting, so Charly knew immediately that the two other Glitter Girls, Hannah and Zoe, had arrived. She rushed to open the door

"Hi everyone!" said Hannah.

Both she and Zoe were wearing their special Glitter Girl jackets. Hannah's mum was a costume designer and she'd made them especially for the Glitter Girls. She'd embroidered the letters "GG" on the back of them in pink and silver thread. The Glitter Girls always wore their jackets when they were doing something cool together.

"Morning!" said Zoe. "Charly, your mum says that she wants to go in ten minutes so please will we all go to the loo and be ready at the front door by then!"

"OK," said Meg. "I'll just take this hair clip off and I'll be ready."

"Oh, isn't that cute?" said Hannah, gently touching the pink monkey clinging to Meg's hair.

"Yeah, it's great!" said Flo. "And just look at all these other slides that Charly's aunt sent her. But I think this monkey's just so cool."

"Monkey!" said a little voice from the doorway, making the girls jump. It was Lily, Charly's cute younger sister. Just like Charly, Lily had blonde hair, but she didn't wear glasses like her older sister.

"Hello Lily!" said Flo, rushing over to pick her up.

Lily giggled. "Time to go!"

"Oops, it's gone nine!" said Zoe, looking at her watch. They'd been so lost in looking at the cool clips that they hadn't been keeping an eye on the time.

"Let's go then, Lily!" said Charly, grabbing her own Glitter Girl jacket and a neat little pink and purple purse that she kept her pocket money in.

"Better hurry!" said Meg, slipping on her own jacket and racing down the stairs behind Charly and Lily.

★ ♥ ★ ♥ ★ ♥ ★

It didn't take that long to get to the shopping centre, and the Glitter Girls chatted away with Lily about the school fête all the way there. They weren't sure that Lily understood anything they were talking about – after all, she was only three. But Lily thought that everything the Glitter Girls said and did was great and she was happy to listen to them, even if she didn't know what it was all about.

Mrs Fisher pulled into a parking place not far from the entrance to the shopping centre, and they all jumped out.

"Now girls, make sure we all stick together! I don't want to lose you – even if it is in Girl's Dream!" She strapped Lily into her buggy and set off towards the shops.

Lily waved her favourite doll, Treena, high in the air.

"Go Glitter!" she giggled at the Glitter Girls.

"Go Glitter" was the Glitter Girls' favourite saying. They said it whenever they thought of a brilliant idea or were setting off to do something super-cool. Even Lily seemed to know that Girl's Dream was a place that they had been dreaming of coming to ever since it had opened.

Straight away, they all raised their hands high above their heads.

"Go Glitter!" they all cheered and smiled.

Chapter 3

It didn't take the Glitter Girls long to find Girl's Dream. The shop was even bigger than they had expected and just looking through the window, they could see that it lived up to its name.

"Just look at all that jewellery!" said Hannah, pointing at a counter that was shimmering in the lights.

The latest *Steps* song was playing as the girls went in.

"I'll be over here with Lily, girls, while you look around, OK?" said Mrs Fisher, heading for the fluffy toys.

"Yes, that's fine," they all replied, as they stood, motionless – amazed at the fantastic things that surrounded them.

"Would you look at those!" said Flo as she headed over towards a nail bar. It didn't take the other Glitter Girls long to follow her over. There was a girl about their age sitting in front of one of the shop assistants, who was wearing a pale pink overall. The girl had her hands spread out on a mat in front of her and she was having her painted nails decorated with tiny pictures of butterflies.

"I've *got* to have those on my fingers!" said Zoe, who was wearing her favourite butterfly clips all over her hair.

"Wow! They are *so* pretty!" admired Charly.

"And look at her!" exclaimed Meg, going over to where another girl was having her hair braided by an assistant who had a bindi on her forehead.

"Now that's for me!" said Hannah, who had gorgeous, long ginger hair. It had taken her ages to grow and she was very proud of it.

"Hey guys – look at those rings!" Flo said,

running over to look at the jewellery in more detail.

There were rings in every colour you can imagine! Some were made up of tiny beads on elastic. Others were silver or gold with glass jewels decorating them. There were hair slides to match – as well as gorgeous sparkly bracelets and necklaces.

"How does this look?" asked Meg, putting a diamond tiara on her head.

"It's lovely!" said Zoe. "But hey! Look at all that gorgeous stationery!"

Quickly, Meg took off the tiara and followed Zoe and the others over to the other side of the shop, where there was a display of journals, pens, pencils, rubbers, rulers – simply everything that any Glitter Girl could want for writing down secrets or letters to each other. Everything matched: the covers of the books and pads sparkled and the swirly patterns shimmered under the lights. Some of the paper was specially scented so it smelled of perfume or flowers. Some of it even had rose petals actually in the paper!

"I've got to have some!" said Charly, fishing in her purse to see how much pocket money she had.

But then there were all the beautiful clothes to look at. There were amazing sequinned T-shirts with matching jeans, embroidered crop tops and black trousers and shirts with diamanté patterns stitched on to them. The Glitter Girls wanted them all! Then there were the books: a cool new series about a group of best friends ("Just like us!" Zoe said), and some wicked books about how to make friendship bracelets and beaded jewellery as well as others about animals and fashion.

Then Charly spotted some wicked photo frames that were made out of pink furry fabric ("I want one!" Meg cried). In the make-up section of the shop, there were so many things that the Glitter Girls couldn't take them all in: little spirally wands of magical colours that you could wave through your hair to make it glisten with colour; glittery gel that you rubbed lightly on to your cheeks to make them sparkle; lip glosses in all kinds of cool and tasty fruity colours and flavours; really amazing bubble baths that were separated into different layers of colour that you could then shake up to make them look like thousands of droplets of a rainbow. Then there were the socks and tights and the pretty pink underwear . . . oh, there was so much! And the Glitter Girls wished they could have all of it!

In the end, after working out how much pocket money they each had to spend, each Glitter Girl paid for a treat that was particularly special to her.

Zoe, of course, had her nails painted and bought some more nail motifs so that she could put some on herself, at home. Hannah had her hair braided and also spent some more pocket money on buying a long dangly tassle of feathers that the assistant showed her how to attach to her hair.

Charly and Meg both bought some lip gloss and some bindis. The assistant even put a bindi on each of their foreheads (a pink glittery one for Meg and a gold one for Charly), so they had an extra one free! And Flo bought herself a set of rings that could either be worn separately or could be intertwined to be made into a pattern all along the length of one finger.

"Come on girls," said Charly's mum, as she and Lily gathered them all together a couple of hours later. "Let's go to the burger bar for lunch!"

"I'm starving," said Meg. "But do we have to go?"

"I think we should," said Charly's mum. "I know I need something to eat and I'm certain that Lily does. Look, she's started to chew her new book!"

Lily's present from Girl's Dream had been a little book that was all about animals. But she was now so hungry that she'd begun to nibble it!

"Puppy!" said Lily, proudly showing off her new treasure in one hand. The other was still clutching Treena – who was now sporting a bindi that one of the assistants had given her!

"Please!" pleaded Charly. "Do we have to go?"

"Afraid so," said her mum, laughing.

"Ohh!" said Hannah, twiddling with the braid in her hair.

"Tell you what, though," said Mrs Fisher, pushing Lily out of the shop. "If you help me to do my other shopping after lunch, we'll go back to Girl's Dream once more before we go home.

"Yes!" the girls all shouted at once, "Go Glitter!"

Chapter 4

Over their lunch in the burger bar, Charly, Hannah, Zoe, Flo and Meg chatted away about their exciting morning in Girl's Dream. And Lily joined in as much as she could too, gibbering away between mouthfuls of lunch and stroking Zoe's painted nails. Lily was certainly a Glitter Girl of the future!

"Girl's Dream is just the most magical place, isn't it?" said Meg, resting her chin in her hands. Like the other Glitter Girls, she'd already eaten her lunch and was now dreaming about all the other things she wanted to save up her pocket money to buy on her next trip to Girl's Dream.

"Certainly is," said Flo, playing with her rings – they looked fantastic.

"Think how many other girls would love to go there!" Zoe marvelled, as she spread her spectacular nails on the table in front of her. She just knew that even her big sisters, Jemma and Beth, were going to be jealous of these nails.

"That's it!" Hannah exploded, flicking her hair back from her face. "You've got it, Zoe!"

"Got what?" Zoe was puzzled.

"The school fête!" Hannah said, as if that explained everything.

"Sorry," said Meg, who was just as puzzled as Zoe, "but what has Girl's Dream got to do with the school fête?"

"Oh, I get it!" said Flo, a smile spreading over her face.

"Will someone please explain?" said Zoe, looking exasperated.

"Well, like Meg said, Girl's Dream is really magical and every girl would like to go there." Hannah seemed to think that that was enough to make Zoe realize what she meant.

Now it was Charly's turn to be puzzled. "Yes, OK! But what's that got to do with the school fête?"

"Well, why don't we have a stall at the school fête that does makeovers? Just like Girl's Dream?" said Flo.

"Exactly!" said Hannah, flicking her hair back again.

"What a brilliant idea!" said Charly, who was busy helping her mum feed Lily her lunch.

"It does sound good," said Mrs Fisher. "I certainly don't remember anything like it before."

"But how could we do it?" said Meg. "I mean, when we did the tombola last year, everyone donated the prizes. We can't ask people to donate bindis and hair braids, can we?"

"No . . . that's true. . ." said Hannah, looking disappointed that her great idea seemed to be over before it had even begun.

"Hold on a minute!" cried Zoe excitedly. "Remember what Mrs Wadhurst said in assembly? She said that some stalls were allowed to have some money to buy in stock so that they could set up for the fête!"

"Yes, she did!" said Meg. "Do you think she'd let us have some money to get going with?"

"Course she will," Flo said, with certainty. "I'm sure she'll see what a good idea it is."

"Well, she might. . ." said Hannah, who didn't feel as confident about it as her friend.

"Well, why don't you talk to the manager of the shop when we go back?" suggested Mrs Fisher. "You can tell her about your idea for a makeover stall, and see what she says. Then, when you go to school on Monday, you could put your ideas to Mrs Wadhurst and see what *she* thinks."

"Brilliant!" said Flo.

"Cool!" agreed Meg and Charly.

"And I know exactly what we could call the stall!" said Zoe, triumphantly, "Magical Makeovers!"

"Go Glitter!" the other girls said in agreement!

★ ♥ ★ ♥ ★ ♥ ★

The Glitter Girls did their best to help Mrs Fisher with the rest of her shopping. Meg and Flo carried the bags, Charly pushed the trolley when they went into the supermarket, and Zoe and Hannah took turns to push Lily's buggy. So it wasn't that long before they were back at Girl's Dream bursting with questions.

As soon as they arrived, Zoe asked one of the assistants if they could speak to the manager of the shop.

A few minutes later, a kind-looking lady called Gina appeared and, with the help of the other Glitter Girls, Zoe explained the idea they had had for the school fête.

"Sounds like a great idea to me," said Gina.

"We could put together a selection of hair braids, nail decorations and varnishes, some bindis and perhaps some body-art temporary tattoos. And perhaps we could put in some lip glosses and sparkly gels for you to sell as well. How does that sound?" Gina smiled at the Glitter Girls.

"It sounds brilliant!" said Hannah, speaking for all the girls at once.

"Now we've just got to persuade Mrs Wadhurst what a great idea it is. She's our headteacher," explained Flo.

"I see," said Gina. "Well, if you think she'll take some persuading, why don't you tell Mrs Wadhurst that we'll give you some vouchers to give to all the customers that come to your stall."

"Vouchers?" asked Meg. "What sort of vouchers?"

"Vouchers offering 50p off a first purchase in Girl's Dream," said Gina.

"Now that sounds even more brilliant!" said Zoe, excitedly.

"It certainly does," said Charly, grinning from ear to ear.

"So, when is the fête?" Gina asked.

"In three weeks' time," said Hannah.

"That's good then," said Gina. "It'll give *us* time to put some goodies together for your Magical Makeovers stall. And it'll give *you* time to get practising on your nail and hair techniques. With a bit of practice, I'm sure you'll all be experts in no time!"

"Brilliant!" said Zoe, thinking of the possibility of practising on Jemma and Beth.

"If it's all right with your mums," said Gina, looking at Mrs Fisher, "you can come back next week to let me know how you get on with Mrs Wadhurst and, if she's said yes, perhaps I could get some help from the other assistants to teach you some of the tricks of painting nails and braiding hair. How does that sound?" Gina asked, smiling at them.

"Go Glitter!" all the girls shouted at once,

punching the air with their fists. It was the first time that Gina had heard the Glitter Girls' enthusiastic catchphrase. But somehow she knew that it wasn't going to be the last!

Chapter 5

The Glitter Girls could hardly bear to wait for the rest of the weekend to be over so that they could speak to Mrs Wadhurst about their Magical Makeovers idea. They had chatted away about all the things they could do on the stall for the entire journey home. Then, they'd rushed back to their families to tell them about the brilliant idea the Glitter Girls had had. Everyone agreed that it sounded like a great plan.

"Girl's Dream is just the *most* fantastic place," Zoe told her sisters. And she went on to tell them all about the make-up and the nail bar.

"Sounds cool," they agreed. "Maybe you could do a makeover on us at the fête."

Hannah's mum had said a similar thing when Hannah had told her all about the hair braiding and stuff.

That night, back home in their own bedrooms, each of the Glitter Girls was already thinking about everything they could do at the Magical Makeovers stall. They desperately hoped that it would happen!

★ ♥ ★ ♥ ★ ♥ ★

"GG!"

Hannah rushed to open her bedroom door and welcome in her friends.

It was Sunday afternoon. Zoe and Charly piled in behind Meg and Flo, deep in discussion about the joint riding lesson they'd had that morning. Flo had also been out for the morning with her family. They'd been to a go-kart racing track and Flo came back looking excited and exhausted after her morning's fun. Flo told all the Glitter Girls about how she'd had the chance to drive the go-kart on her own for a couple of races. She'd even managed to come second in one of them! Flo wanted to be a rally driver when she left school and she was always desperate for an excuse to get behind the wheel of any vehicle she might be allowed to drive.

But with the excitement of go-karts left behind, Flo was more than happy to practise painting everyone's nails, except for Zoe's – hers were still looking perfect from the day before. And Zoe practised her braiding skills on Meg's and Charly's hair.

"Now that's *cool*!" Charly said, admiring her hair when Zoe had finished.

"Don't you just love this colour?" Hannah asked, waving her newly painted nails at her friends.

"Careful you don't smudge it!" Meg winced. "You know Gina said that nails take as long as half an hour to dry properly!"

The other Glitter Girls laughed. "Trust you to get us organized, Meg!" Flo giggled.

"Well. . ." Meg was frowning at first, but then she collapsed into laughter with her friends. "OK! But I just like things done properly!"

After a great afternoon of makeover fun, the Glitter Girls finally had to make their way to their own homes, to get ready for the next week at school. And to get ready to speak to Mrs Wadhurst about Magical Makeovers.

"There's just one problem," Meg said, as the girls were putting on their jackets, ready to go home.

"What's that?" Flo asked.

"These nails!" Meg said, admiring her beautifully polished and shiny nails.

"Why?" Hannah wondered.

"Well," Meg looked at the others. "We can't go to school with our nails painted, can we?"

"Oh no!" the Glitter Girls groaned. . .

★ ♥ ★ ♥ ★ ♥ ★

On Monday morning the Glitter Girls went back to school, bursting with news to tell Mrs Wadhurst and their teacher, Miss Stanley.

As soon as the bell went, they hurried into class. Miss Stanley was at her table, doing some marking.

"Morning, girls!" Miss Stanley looked up at them. "Goodness, you look pleased with yourselves. What have you been up to?"

Before she could say another word, the Glitter Girls started to tell her all about Girl's Dream and their great idea for the fête.

"So, you see, we've got everything organized, Miss Stanley!" said Meg, confidently.

"All we've got to do is go to Girl's Dream and fetch the stuff," confirmed Flo.

"I think," said Miss Stanley, "that perhaps you need to talk to Mrs Wadhurst about it. I mean, I agree, girls, it does sound like a very good plan. But Mrs Wadhurst is in charge of all the stalls for the school fête, so it might be a good idea to get her to give you the go-ahead before you get too carried away, don't you think?"

Miss Stanley smiled kindly at the Glitter Girls. She knew how much the girls liked having adventures and how everything they did wasn't just fun for them but usually fun for other people, too. Only last term, the Glitter Girls had helped out at the local hospital radio when they'd been DJs on a programme for the children's ward. They had called their show *Glitter FM* and it had been such a success that they'd been asked back quite a few times since to present some more shows.

"OK, Miss Stanley," sighed Charly. "We'll talk to Mrs Wadhurst."

"Yes, but when?" asked Zoe, who was always in a hurry to get on with things.

"I'll ask Mrs Wadhurst if she can spare a couple of minutes at breaktime," said Miss Stanley. "In the meantime, back to your chairs please, girls, because it's time for us to take the register and get on with our reading."

★ ♥ ★ ♥ ★ ♥ ★

As soon as the bell went for break, Miss Stanley called Charly, Zoe, Hannah, Meg and Flo over to her. "I sent a message about your idea to Mrs Wadhurst earlier and she's just sent one back saying that she can talk to you for five minutes now."

"Great!" cried Flo, grabbing Meg by the arm in excitement.

"Well, go on then!" said Miss Stanley. "Mrs Wadhurst can't wait all day for you! And good luck, girls!"

The Glitter Girls didn't need telling twice. They raced out of their classroom towards Mrs Wadhurst's office.

Mrs Wadhurst was waiting for the girls. She was used to their adventures and schemes and was wondering what their latest idea might be all about. Miss Stanley had only told her that it was something to do with the school fête.

"Well, you see, Mrs Wadhurst," began Flo, pushing her dark hair away from her face, "we wondered if we could run a kind of beauty bar."

"You know," said Zoe, "nail painting and decorating, hair braids – that sort of stuff."

"And body art – tattoos. . ." added Meg.

". . .bindis, jewellery. . ." Hannah said.

". . .make-up," Charly finished.

Then Zoe explained how Gina at Girl's Dream had offered to help them out – and that they needed some help with the money to buy the initial things.

"I see," Mrs Wadhurst said thoughtfully. "I must say it does sound like you've done a lot of thinking about this. So you would need some money to buy the basic materials for the stall?"

"Yes, Mrs Wadhurst," the Glitter Girls all said at once, feeling nervous about their idea for the first time. After all, no one had ever run a stall like Magical Makeovers at a school fête before.

"Well, I suppose it would be different," said

Mrs Wadhurst, smiling at them. "Perhaps we should give it a try."

"Yes!" said Charly and Meg at the same time.

"Thanks, Mrs Wadhurst!" said the other three.

"What are you going to call your stall, girls?" asked Mrs Wadhurst.

"Magical Makeovers," explained Hannah.

"That sounds good, but before I give you a definite yes, can you write me a list of all the things you'll have to buy to set up your stall? And an idea of how much money it will all cost."

"Oh. . ." Flo didn't know what to say. Did this mean that the Glitter Girls weren't going to get their chance after all?

Charly and Hannah looked at the others, feeling equally as worried.

But Meg and Zoe realized exactly how they could make Magical Makeovers happen.

"No problem, Mrs Wadhurst. We can do a list for you for tomorrow," Meg said confidently.

The other Glitter Girls looked at her in relief. Trust Meg to be so organized!

"Excellent, Meg," Mrs Wadhurst smiled and looked at her watch. "Now, you'd better get off because I've got a meeting with someone," she said. "Bye bye."

"Bye!" all the Glitter Girls said at once. "Thank you Mrs Wadhurst."

The Glitter Girls piled out of Mrs Wadhurst's office and closed the door behind them.

As soon as they were outside in the playground, they exploded with excitement. Another of their adventures was about to begin!

"Go Glitter!"

Chapter 6

At lunchtime, the Glitter Girls couldn't stop talking about Magical Makeovers.

"We'll need to do some posters," said Hannah. "Then we can put them up around school to tell everyone about the stall."

"Good idea," agreed Zoe. "Flo, do you think you could do those? You're so good at art."

"No problem," said Flo, who was more than happy to say yes. "I might even get Kim to help me." Kim was Flo's big sister. She was even more brilliant at art than Flo was.

"Great," said Meg. "Now – what are we going to sell on the stall?"

"How about some hair stuff?" Hannah suggested. "You know, scrunchies and things?"

"Yes!" Charly agreed. "We could make some out of bright-coloured fabric."

"And we could sew beads and feathers on them!" said Zoe.

"OK," said Meg, taking a tiny pink notebook out of her skirt pocket. It had a tiny pencil attached to it on a piece of ribbon. "Let's start a list." And Meg started to write in her book.

"And we'll need some nail varnish, won't we?" Zoe suggested. "If we're going to do nail art."

"And some of that glittery make-up gel," added Flo.

"What about body-art stuff as well?" asked Hannah.

"Yes!" said Meg, still busily jotting things down in her book. "We'll need to have some of that gel ink that Gina showed us as well as those tattoo transfers."

"Could we sell little bars of soap, too? You know – little things like that make great treats and presents for people," suggested Zoe.

"Good idea!" said Flo.

"OK," said Meg. "We'll have to speak to Gina about it, won't we? Now, how are we going to organize who does what?"

"Well, I think that Zoe and Charly should do the hair braids and stuff," said Hannah, tucking a stray wisp of her own long red hair behind her ear. "I mean, you're both so good at plaiting pony tails and things – you'll be great at it."

"Too right!" agreed Flo. "Good idea, Hannah."

So that was decided, but the Glitter Girls had lots of other things to make plans about and they agreed to meet up at Meg's house after school that day.

As the girls made their way back into their classroom, Meg whispered, "And just you wait and see what my dad's bought me to help with my cello practice! You won't believe it until you see it!"

★ ♥ ★ ♥ ★ ♥ ★

At four o'clock that afternoon, Charly, Flo, Zoe and Hannah arrived at Meg's house. Meg and her mum were busy getting some refreshments ready for the Glitter Girls' meeting. While they were in the kitchen, Charly led the way upstairs to Meg's bedroom.

"So what do you think Meg's new present is?" Flo wondered out loud to the others.

"Maybe it's a music case?" Hannah asked.

"Or a new cello?" Zoe suggested.

Once inside Meg's room though, the Glitter Girls realized they were wrong. Sitting next to Meg's bed was her cello, still inside its case. But next to that was the most gorgeous music stand that had ever existed! It was gorgeous because it was bright pink! Not only was it bright pink, but it was translucent too!

"Wow!" said Charly, who saw it first.

"Wow what?" asked Flo, as she bundled into the room behind her. "Oh wow. . ." she finished as she saw the music stand, in all its pink glory.

Zoe and Hannah came in behind the other two and stopped dead in their tracks.

"It's fantastic!" said Hannah.

"It's wicked!" said Zoe, stroking the music stand.

Just then, Meg and her mum came into the bedroom. They were holding trays stacked with pizza slices, popcorn and cool drinks.

"So you've spotted my present then?" said Meg, smiling.

Meg was absolutely mad about all kinds of music and she had posters about music and musicians all over her bedroom walls. Like the other Glitter Girls, Meg's bedroom was painted pink. All of them were really proud of their bedrooms and spent lots of time making things for their rooms and finding pink and glittery accessories to make them look even more special.

"My dad found it in a music shop in London. Isn't it great? I needed a music stand and he said they just happened to have that one."

Meg's mum put her tray of goodies down on the floor and smiled at the Glitter Girls.

"Well, I'll leave you girls to have your meeting. Let me know if there is anything you need, won't you? I'll be downstairs getting tea ready for Jack and Sue. Bye for now," said Mrs Morgan, closing the door behind her.

Even the pink music stand was no competition for the delicious pizza after a busy day at school. As soon as the food was in front of them, the girls dived in.

"So," said Zoe, between mouthfuls, "what else do we need to decide?" Zoe was always good at getting the Glitter Girls' adventures going.

"I was thinking that I'd like to do the body art and tattoos and things, if that's OK with everyone else?" said Hannah.

"Sounds fine," said Charly. "If Zoe and I are doing the hair, that leaves Flo and Meg to do the nails and sell the make-up things."

"Bags I do the nails!" Flo pleaded.

"And I want to do the money. I've always wanted to run a shop!" said Meg, smiling.

She was always the most organized of the Glitter Girls and the others knew that, out of all of them, Meg would be the best one to take the money and keep a record of everything.

"Well, that's all those bits sorted," said Meg. "We've just got to go back to Girl's Dream on Saturday to talk to Gina. Then we can get practising!"

"Yes!" said Flo. "It's going to be great, isn't it?" She hugged her knees, thinking of all the fun the Glitter Girls were going to have at the school summer fête.

"Tell you what," said Flo. "Why don't we have another go at some nails now?"

Chapter 7

The rest of the week just flew by. The Glitter Girls met up after school every night so they could plan exactly how they wanted the Magical Makeovers stand to look. It didn't take long to decide that they wanted to decorate the stand in pink from top to bottom. So, one afternoon, the girls arranged to go to Hannah's house and spend some time with her mum in her workroom.

"Now, we've got to look for something we can drape over the stand to make it look special, haven't we?" Hannah's mum asked, while she rummaged in a basket stuffed full of exotic materials.

"We'll need something to cover the table as well," said Meg.

"OK," said Hannah's mum. "I've got an idea. . ." She rummaged some more and then finally pulled some fabric out from the bottom of the basket. "How's this?"

She held the material up for the girls to see.

When the Glitter Girls saw it, they gasped in amazement.

"It's just beautiful!" Flo spluttered.

And it was. Not only was the material a gorgeous shade of bright pink, but it had thousands of tiny silken silver threads running right through it. So when you looked at the material from one way it looked pink, but as it moved and caught the light, the material shimmered with silver. It was just perfect for the Glitter Girls.

"Well, that sounds like it's sorted," Hannah's mum smiled at the girls. "And after the fête perhaps we can see about making some bags or something out of the fabric."

"Ooh! Cool!" Charly said.

Hannah's mum made costumes for the theatre and was always making the Glitter Girls lovely things from leftover fabric. It was Hannah's mum who had made the special denim jackets that the Glitter Girls always wore when they were together.

"Great," Hannah said, feeling really proud of her mum.

"Hey!" exclaimed Meg. "Do you think we could make some cute little rucksacks?"

"That would be perfect!" said Zoe.

"OK," said Hannah's mum, already picturing what the bags could look like. "I'll see what I can do."

Of course, there were other things that the Glitter Girls needed for the stand. They decided that they should have baskets to put all the special makeover things in, so all the girls asked their friends and family if they had any baskets they could borrow. But they still didn't have enough. Luckily, Flo came up with a great idea.

The girls were in town one afternoon after school and as they were passing the florist's, Flo had a brainwave. She went in and asked if the girls could borrow some big flower baskets from them.

"Well," said the lady in the shop, "I think I might just have something for you at the back. Do you mind waiting here a minute?"

"OK!" the girls all said at once. A short while later, the lady came back in with a selection of big baskets with great hooped handles. They were decorated with pink ribbon, tied into huge pink bows. They looked gorgeous and the Glitter Girls knew immediately that they would look absolutely perfect decorating the table at the front of the stand.

"Cool!" said Charly, taking two of the baskets from the lady.

"They're great!" agreed Zoe.

"Thanks!" said Hannah.

"So, they'll do then?" the lady laughed.

"They're perfect!" said Meg.

"Fantastic!" Flo exclaimed. "Thanks so much!"

"Yes, thanks!" said the others.

"They're only on loan," said the lady. "We'll need them back when it's over."

"No problem!" said Meg. "And we'll make sure that we tell everyone you helped us."

"Go Glitter!" the girls all said.

★ ♥ ★ ♥ ★ ♥ ★

Later in the week, Flo and her sister Kim made the best posters ever. Kim had drawn all the lettering and outline pictures on all of them and Flo had helped her with the colour.

COME AND HAVE A MAGICAL MAKEOVER AT THE SCHOOL FÊTE! the posters read. They were brilliant – painted with fluorescent inks and dotted all over with glitter. As soon as they were finished, the Glitter Girls immediately started to put them up all over the school.

"I had a word with the man in the corner shop," said Flo. "He said that he would put one up in the window.

"Great," Hannah said.

"Yes, everyone will see it there," Meg agreed.

And so the week whizzed by. Zoe and Charly spent every available moment practising doing plaits. They did them on the ponies that they rode at their riding lessons. They plaited each other's hair. They even dug out their old Barbies and plaited their hair. They also tried out lots of funky new hairstyles that they copied from the models in some magazines. Zoe tried doing lots of tiny plaits in Charly's hair and Charly experimented with putting Zoe's hair into two cute little topknots – she looked excellent!

Hannah got practising on doing her body art. Her little brother, Joe, was happy to let Hannah draw all over him in felt pen as she practised the patterns that she would draw with the special body-art gel ink that they had seen at Girl's Dream. Unfortunately, Hannah's mum wasn't so happy when she saw Joe covered in ink! Hannah had to say sorry to her mum and help to wash off all the felt pen. It did come off in the end – but it took quite a bit of scrubbing (and moaning from Joe!). Hannah decided that she would wait to practise some more at the weekend with Gina at Girl's Dream.

So, it was a busy week for the Glitter Girls. But they enjoyed every minute of it. And they couldn't wait for Saturday to arrive so that they could go back to Girl's Dream and really get Magical Makeovers on the road!

Chapter 8

BRRIIIIINGGGG!

Hannah rushed to open the front door and managed to get there just before her brother.

Charly, Zoe, Meg and Flo piled noisily into the house, chattering excitedly. The Glitter Girls were off to Girl's Dream again for a Magical Makeovers session with Gina, and they couldn't wait.

They made their way straight to Hannah's bedroom. Hannah's mum had made Hannah lots of beautiful things for her room to make it extra glitzy. On her bed was a bedspread made of lots of different materials which Hannah's mum had sewn together in a random patch-work pattern. Some of the fabrics were shimmery with metallic threads and some had embroidery on them. Above Hannah's bed was a canopy made of the finest, floaty gauze – it looked like something out of a fairy tale. The curtains were made of a deep pink fabric and there was a selection of pictures on the walls, all in pink, purple and silver frames. Talk about Girl's Dream – Hannah's bedroom was a Glitter Girl's dream!

"So," said Zoe. "What's the plan of action then?"

"Well, my mum is going to be ready to take us to the shopping centre in a minute," Hannah replied. "Mrs Wadhurst has given Mum some money to buy the things we need for the stall. Mum rang Gina earlier in the week and arranged for us to stay for a couple of hours at Girl's Dream so that we can learn all of Gina's make-up tricks," said Hannah excitedly.

"Fantastic!" said Meg, grinning from ear to ear.

"I can't wait!" agreed Flo.

"Brilliant," said Zoe.

"Let's just go!" said Charly, as impatient as the others.

"Go Glitter!" everyone else replied!

As soon as they were at Girl's Dream, the Glitter Girls started searching for their favourite accessories.

"I can see exactly why you were all so desperate to get here!" said Hannah's mum. "This place is fantastic! I just wish it was somewhere for me to be too!"

The Glitter Girls laughed.

"Isn't it wicked?" agreed Flo. "We love it here."

"Well, I'll leave you lot here with Gina then," Hannah's mum smiled at Gina, who was all ready to get the girls going. "Joe and I will go off to the Crazy Crocodile Club."

The Crazy Crocodile Club was one of Joe's favourite places. It was a kind of super-adventure playground full of climbing frames and slides. There was waterless swimming, trampolines and all kinds of other activities.

Hannah's mum smiled at Joe. "I just hope that I'm going to have as much fun today as you and the Glitter Girls are! See you girls later! Bye Gina!"

"Bye!" the Glitter Girls called.

"Now," said Gina. "Let's get started."

★ ♥ ★ ♥ ★ ♥ ★

Charly and Zoe had a fantastic time learning how to wrap braids into hair. They practised on Hannah because she had such lovely long, thick hair.

"This is great!" Hannah said, admiring her ginger tresses in the mirror when her friends had finished.

"Do you like it then?" Charly asked.

"Like it?" Hannah flicked at her fringe with her fingers. "I love it!"

Later, Charly and Zoe even learned how to weave feathers and strips of neon fake hair in amongst the real hair to give truly spectacular effects! Gina spent ages with the pair of them and after the first hour of practising told them that she thought they could come back and get a job doing hair weaving any time they wanted! The two girls smiled with pride.

In the meantime, Flo was with a girl called Sarah. She was one of Gina's assistants and she knew everything about painting nails and putting decorations on them.

"What do you think of these?" Flo asked Meg, showing her her own toenails. She'd stuck tiny diamantés on her big toenails. They were perfect for peeping through the toes of her sandals!

"They are so cool," Meg sighed, wishing she had toenails like that too.

Hannah spent her time with another of Gina's assistants called Samantha and she was busy perfecting body art. She was just brilliant at it –

obviously all that practise with felt pens on her brother had paid off! With Samantha's help, Hannah "tattooed" Meg's shoulder with a tiny little pink daisy.

"Wow!" Charly and Zoe said when they saw it.

"Can you do one for me?" Flo asked.

"And me!" Zoe asked.

"Sure!" Hannah said, smiling. "As long as you pay me for it at the Magical Makeovers stall!"

In-between her modelling work, Meg had a great time selecting lip and cheek glosses and nail polishes with an assistant called Carrie. Together, they selected lots of different colours – some bright, some pale, some glittery, some just shimmery – and placed them in tiny little transparent cellophane bags. Then they secured the tops of the bags with bright pink ribbon, on to which they threaded the Girl's Dream vouchers that Gina had spoken about. Carrie even showed Meg how to make the ribbons twist and curl by running the back of a pair of scissors along them. Once the bags were ready, Carrie and Meg put them into two enormous baskets and sat back to admire their work.

It was at exactly that moment that Hannah's mum and Joe arrived back at Girl's Dream. The Glitter Girls couldn't believe that two hours had already passed!

"Hey, what amazing baskets, Meg!" said Mrs Giles. "And look at that shoulder!" She gazed around the shop at the other Glitter Girls. "Just look at your lovely hair, Hannah! And yours as well, Zoe. Fabulous nails, Flo. And look at yours too, Charly!" Flo had practised on Charly's fingernails as well.

"It can't be time to go already!" Zoe exclaimed.

"Afraid so, girls!" smiled Hannah's mum. "Come on, I'll take you all to lunch."

"Do we have to go?" pleaded Hannah and Meg.

"Come on," Hannah's mum said kindly. "Joe is

starving and I'm sure that once you girls think about it, you are too! Let's go off and have lunch."

Reluctantly, the Glitter Girls started to put on their special jackets and grab their bags.

Laden with armfuls of baskets, the girls made their way to the door.

"Wait there girls, while I sort out the payment for all these goodies," said Mrs Giles.

"Hasn't this been great?" Charly asked all of her friends.

"Excellent!" Flo agreed.

"Seriously cool!" added Hannah.

"Really wicked!" Meg and Zoe said together, and laughed.

"Thanks so much for all your help, Gina," said Charly.

"Yes, thanks Gina," chorused the rest of the Glitter Girls.

"No problem, girls," said Gina. "Good luck with everything, and make sure you come back and tell me all about it!"

"We will," said Meg excitedly, smiling at her friends.

Now the Magical Makeovers had really begun!

Chapter 9

The Glitter Girls spent the next week in a whirl of meetings about their Magical Makeovers stall.

Like Hannah's mum, Charly's was also good at sewing, and on Monday afternoon after school, she joined the Glitter Girls when they all met up in Mrs Giles's workroom. Hannah's mum had had a great idea for extra things that the Glitter Girls could sell on their stall: hair scrunchies made out of a selection of fabrics she had leftover from making costumes for a musical show called *Tropical Island*. All the fabrics were fantastically bold shades of pink, purple and orange and Charly, Hannah, Meg, Flo and Zoe all agreed that they would make really pretty scrunchies.

It didn't take the girls long to learn how the scrunchies were made and after an hour of chatting and busy sewing, there was soon quite a big pile of scrunchies – some velvety, some plain and some patterned with little flowers – on the work table in front of them.

"Well," said Hannah's mum, looking at her watch, "I think that's a job well done, don't you?"

"I certainly do," agreed Charly's mum. "Do you think you girls are ready for some tea?"

"Yes please!" the girls all called back.

"Give me a few minutes then, and we'll see what we can rustle up," said Mrs Giles, and she and Charly's mum went downstairs.

"What are we going to put these in?" Meg asked no one in particular. She was looking at the pile of scrunchies and deciding which one she was going to buy for herself.

"Let's decorate a box for them," suggested

Zoe, as they'd run out of space in the flower baskets. "We could get a couple of small boxes from the local shop and cover them in wrapping paper and things. Like we did for *Glitter FM*."

"Oh, you mean like the Request Box?" asked Flo.

"Great idea!" agreed Meg. "We could do that tomorrow."

"And we can finish the posters at the same time," said Hannah.

"TEA, GIRLS!" called a voice from downstairs.

"Go Glitter!" they all said.

And the Glitter Girls were off.

★ ♥ ★ ♥ ★ ♥ ★

The following afternoon, the Glitter Girls met up as planned. They decorated a box for the scrunchies and finished off the posters. Over the next few days, they went round all the shops in town, asking the shopkeepers if they would put up posters telling everyone about Magical Makeovers.

By the end of the week, there couldn't have been anyone left in the area who didn't know that Magical Makeovers was going to be at the school summer fête!

In fact, by Friday, the Glitter Girls were too excited to sit down and just wait for Saturday to arrive. So they all stayed at Zoe's house for a sleepover so that they could get themselves ready for the fête.

Zoe's two older sisters, Beth and Jemma, joined them in Zoe's room. The Glitter Girls were busily trying out their outfits for the next day.

"Hey, that's a great dress, Meg," Hannah said admiringly.

"Thanks – I love your trousers too," Meg replied.

"You're all going to look great!" said Beth.

"Course you are!" Jemma agreed.

"OK, so who's going to do my nails then?" Beth asked.

"And who's going to braid my hair?" Jemma wondered.

The Glitter Girls set to it! Between them, they painted and decorated Jemma's and Beth's nails and plaited their hair, as well as giving themselves makeovers too!

"I think I've remembered how Sarah told me to do it," Flo said, as she applied daisies to Beth's nails.

"Hey, cool!" Beth said, admiring her gorgeous fingernails as Flo moved on to Jemma's.

Meantime, Charly plaited Meg's hair. "What do you think of these feathers?" she asked.

"Perfect!" said Flo.

"Yes, I really like them," Meg agreed.

Hannah was busy applying a tattoo to Jemma's shoulder. Jemma was trying desperately to see what was going on, but couldn't get to see it exactly.

"Hey, pass me that mirror Beth!" she called to her sister. Beth handed it over straight away and Jemma held the mirror at an angle so that she could see Hannah at work. "Cute!" Jemma said when the daisy was finished.

"You know, you girls are going to look so fantastic tomorrow that everyone who visits the fête is going to see you and come over for their own Magical Makeover," Beth said.

"Go Glitter!" they all cried.

★ ♥ ★ ♥ ★ ♥ ★

By the end of the evening, the Glitter Girls really did look amazing and Beth and Jemma agreed that Magical Makeovers should be the hit of the fête.

"Hey, you girls," said Jemma, "you make sure you get your beauty sleep, won't you?"

"And you'd better wipe that glitter stuff and mascara off your faces too!" added Beth. "You don't want to put people off with black smudgy eyes in the morning, do you?"

Beth and Jemma left the Glitter Girls to their sleepover. The Glitter Girls washed and brushed their teeth before climbing into their PJs. Then they stumbled around finding their sleeping bags and mattresses that were strewn across the floor.

"It's going to be good tomorrow, isn't it?" Zoe said, yawning.

"Yes!" the others all agreed together.

Only minutes later, the Glitter Girls were fast asleep!

Chapter 10

It was Magical Makeovers day! Charly, Meg, Flo, Hannah and Zoe jumped out of bed as soon as they were awakened by Zoe's dad.

"Morning, girls," he said, poking his head around the door of Zoe's bedroom. There were Glitter Girls all over the place! Zoe and Meg were in the two bunk beds and the other three were in sleeping bags all over the floor. "Time you were up and having breakfast. There's lots for us to do!"

After a rushed breakfast of blueberry muffins, which Zoe's dad had made as a special treat, the Glitter Girls hurried back up to Zoe's room to put on the clothes that they had specially chosen for Magical Makeovers day.

Hannah was wearing a pair of pink flowery pedal pushers with a matching T-shirt. She even had a pair of flip-flops decorated with flowers to wear with them.

Charly had a shimmery bright pink skirt on and a groovy purple short-sleeved shirt.

Flo looked cool in a pair of purple shorts that she had recently been given for her birthday and her Glitter Girls T-shirt.

Meg was wearing a dress covered in a geometric pattern of pink, purple and silvery swirls.

Zoe had chosen to wear some pink dungarees that her sisters had given her. Once, the dungarees had fitted them, but Zoe was pleased that they now fitted her at last.

"Do you think it's going to rain?" Hannah asked anxiously, looking out of Zoe's bedroom window.

"It couldn't!" said Flo in dismay. A rainy day would just ruin the school fête!

"It wouldn't dare!" said Charly.

"No way – not on Magical Makeovers day!" agreed Meg.

"Still, we'd better take our Glitter Girl jackets, don't you think?" suggested Zoe. "In case it gets cold?"

"Good idea," the others agreed, grabbing them and running downstairs.

Out in the garage, the Glitter Girls had assembled everything that they needed for their stall: the fabric for covering the front, back and table; the baskets filled with the little gift bags of gloss and polish; the scrunchies that Hannah's mum delivered the previous night; a pink money-tin for Meg. Then, of course, there were all the things that the Glitter Girls had collected from Girl's Dream: the braids, feathers and body art stuff that they had neatly divided up into carefully marked boxes.

With the help of Jemma and Beth, the Glitter Girls had soon loaded up Zoe's parents' two cars with their things.

"I think you Glitter Girls can come with me!" said Zoe's mum, closing the garage door.

"And we'll go with Dad," agreed Jemma, as she and Beth got into their dad's car.

"See you there!" Beth waved.

"Ready girls?" Dr Baker asked.

"Go Glitter!" the girls shouted back excitedly, their arms held high in the air.

★ ♥ ★ ♥ ★ ♥ ★

Ten minutes later, Dr Baker pulled into the school car park. The fête was being held on the playing field. All around them, people were already getting their stalls ready. The refreshment stall was decorated with balloons and garlands and was laden with bottles of juice and slices of fruit. There was a lucky dip, a book stall, a bottle stall and a craft stall. And over on the other side of the field, the school country-dancing team were practising their line-dance routines. There was a French-food stall being set up alongside a number of stalls where there were all sorts of games to play, like pretend fishing and a coconut shy. The school fête was obviously going to be a great day for all of them!

"This is our place!" said Zoe, running over to a huge sun umbrella. Underneath the umbrella were little tables and chairs.

It was a perfect place for the Magical Makeovers stall, right in the middle of the field. Everyone would be able to see the Glitter Girls' stall the very minute that they came through the gates into the fête!

"Well, let's get going then!" said Zoe. "There's only half an hour before it starts!"

"Doesn't that look fantastic, girls!" said Mrs Wadhurst. She had come round to inspect all of the stalls, just before the fête opened.

The Glitter Girls stood back from their frantic

chores and smiled with pride. It was absolutely true, the Magical Makeovers stall *did* look fantastic.

"Well, have fun today, girls! And enjoy yourselves!" said Mrs Wadhurst, as she set off to check on the other stalls.

"Come on girls, let's take a photo before you begin!" said Zoe's mum, taking her camera out of her bag.

Instantly, Charly, Zoe, Meg, Flo and Hannah stood in line and threw their arms above their heads.

"Go Glitter!"

Seconds later the school bell rang out. The fête had begun!

Within minutes, people were pouring through the school gates, heading for their favourite stalls. All around, games were being played, food and drink was being bought, and money exchanged for crafts and books. The music for the line-dancing filled the air and crowds gathered to watch. And at the Glitter Girls' stall there was already a long queue of girls and their mums waiting for their Magical Makeovers.

"Hey, can you believe this?" Zoe asked the others.

"No!" said Hannah. "But I love it!"

"Isn't it great?" Flo agreed.

"It's already even better than I'd hoped for!" said Charly.

"Come on, you lot!" said Meg, organizing everyone. "Let's get on with it."

For the next hour the girls worked solidly. Hannah was working so hard at decorating people with tattoos and painting gel that she was worried at one point that she might run out of them!

The hair braids and decorations were a huge success and everyone was pleased with them.

Charly and Zoe were enjoying every minute of it too!

Flo had so many people's nails to do that sometimes she was doing two people's at once, so that one girl was sitting waiting for hers to dry while the other one was having her nails decorated!

"Right, don't move, because your nails aren't quite dry yet!" she told one girl from Year 2, who was grinning from ear to ear at the sight of her spangly fingers. "Now, what colour would you like yours?" she asked the little girl's mum.

And while all this was happening, Meg was doing a roaring trade.

"That'll be 50p please!" she said, taking someone's money for a hair scrunchie.

There was no time to stop for any lunch – and hardly any time to talk to each other! – but Jemma and Beth came over to give the girls a snack and some juice. With Meg's sister Sue, they also helped out with some of the makeovers. There were just too many people for even the Glitter Girls to keep up with!

By half past four, the crowds had thinned out and the Glitter Girls found themselves doing the last of their makeovers. It was then that a reporter arrived from the local newspaper.

"Haven't I seen you girls before?" she asked, as she sat down to have her nails done. "In the paper?"

She certainly had! When the Glitter Girls had presented *Glitter FM*, the hospital had sent a photo of them to the paper and they'd been on the front page.

"Yes," said Flo, as she carefully applied a coat of glittery polish. "When we helped out on the hospital radio station."

"That's right! I remember you. You're the Glitter Girls! Well, perhaps you'd like to tell me about this latest idea of yours. Hey, just a minute!" She took her hands carefully away from Flo and ever so gently took out a tiny tape recorder from her bag. "I'll just switch this on to record what we talk about. Then I'll have everything when I go to write it up for the paper."

The Glitter Girls were more than happy to tell her about Magical Makeovers. Each of them told the reporter about what they'd been doing that day.

"And I know it doesn't look quite so good now," said Meg, looking around at the empty baskets and the rubbish bag full of debris, "but it did look great earlier on."

"Well, I think it still looks good – I love all the pink things that you've decorated your stall with," said the reporter, admiring her nails. "And I did come by earlier, but you were so busy no one had time to talk to me so I just took a photo of your stall. It looked fabulous. A great success, judging by all the people who were queuing up!"

She checked to see if her nails were dry and then she handed her money to Meg. "Well, thank you for my nails, Flo. These are going to make everyone jealous back at the paper on Monday! Don't forget to look out for next week's paper," she said. "We're going to have a double-page spread all about the fête!"

"Brilliant!" said Flo.

"Now, I'd better get over to see the ponies before they head off home to their stables. Bye!"

"Bye," the Glitter Girls called, as she walked over to the other side of the field where one of the ponies was taking a smiling little boy for a short trot.

"Phew!" said Flo, sinking down into a chair. It looked as if the newspaper reporter had been their last customer. The playing field was empty now except for all the boys and girls who were running stalls.

"Any chance you've got a moment to do my nails, girls?"

It was Mrs Wadhurst. She'd come for a Magical Makeover! And between them the

Glitter Girls set to, to transform their headteacher into a Glitter Girl just like them!

★ ♥ ★ ♥ ★ ♥ ★

With the last satisfied customer tranformed by Magical Makeovers, it was finally time to pack up. As the Glitter Girls put everything away and took down the last of their posters, Meg counted out the money in the tin.

"Hey!" she said as she piled up the last of the money. "Guess what!"

"Tell us!" said Zoe anxiously.

"Is it more than we made last year?" Hannah asked.

"Go on, tell us!" said Charly, hurrying over.

"Well, after I've taken away the float money that Mrs Wadhurst gave us – and the money we borrowed to buy all the bits and pieces from Girl's Dream," said Meg grinning.

"Come on!" Zoe urged her friend.

"Yes, tell us!" said Hannah.

"Well, we've made a hundred pounds more than we did last year!" Zoe said ecstatically.

"Go Glitter!" the girls said, jumping up and down with joy.

★ ♥ ★ ♥ ★ ♥ ★

At Monday's assembly, Mrs Wadhurst was quick to congratulate everyone for their contributions to the school fête.

"And don't forget to look in the newspaper on Wednesday to see all the photographs!"

How could the Glitter Girls forget? School seemed pretty dull after the excitement of the fête and when the girls met up after school that day, they chilled out in Charly's room, reliving the actual day.

"I can't believe I painted so many nails!" Flo said.

"I plaited so much hair that my fingers ached by the end!" Charly said, flexing her fingers as she spoke.

"And did you see that Mrs Wadhurst still had her nail polish on today?" Hannah asked.

"Too bad she wouldn't let you braid her hair though!" Meg giggled.

"Now that would have been cool!" Zoe agreed.

"Come on. I'm hungry – and I'm sure I'm not the only one!" Charly said. "Let's go and see if my mum will let us bake a cake!"

"Go Glitter!" the girls said, and bundled down the stairs.

★ ♥ ★ ♥ ★ ♥ ★

As soon as they got home on Wednesday, the Glitter Girls rushed to the local shop to buy the paper. There was a photo of Charly, Meg, Hannah, Flo and Zoe at their stall, beneath the Magical Makeovers sign. Underneath the photo, the caption read:

THE GLITTER GIRLS SHINE AGAIN!

Following the success of their hospital radio programme, *Glitter FM*, the Glitter Girls were the stars of the fête with their Magical Makeovers stall. What adventure will the girls get up to next?

"I wonder what our next adventure will be?" said Meg.

"Whatever it is, it's bound to be good!" said Hannah.

"Yes – it'll be cool!" agreed Flo.

"And fun!" added Charly.

"And glittery!" finished Zoe.

"Go Glitter!" they all shouted at once!

Don't miss:

Disco Divas

Charly and Zoe bundled into Meg's bedroom, each carrying a plateful of sandwiches that Meg's mum had given them. None of them wasted any time before in tucking in!

Meg was the most organized of the Glitter Girls. Her room was always neat and tidy. Her mum never had to nag her to sort it out! She played the cello and in her room she kept the most scrumptious translucent pink music stand. None of the other Glitter Girls played an instrument (apart from the recorder, like everyone else at school), but all of them wanted to have the music stand!

"Great hair!" Zoe said, looking at Meg and Hannah.

Meg had long, wavy blonde hair and Hannah had created a mass of tiny plaits all around her head too. She'd even woven in some pretty ribbons amongst the strands of hair.

"It's wicked, isn't it?" said Meg, smiling. "Hannah did it."

"Wow, Hannah!" said Charly. "You haven't forgotten the Magical Makeovers stuff then! Will you do mine again soon?"

Hannah was pretty pleased with it herself and she smiled with satisfaction. "Course," she said. "So, how was your riding lesson?"

"Cool!" Charly replied. "We did some little jumps today, didn't we?"

"Yes – it was really good!" Zoe replied. "And we heard all about some new donkeys that have arrived at the Donkey Sanctuary, too!"

The Donkey Sanctuary was one of the Glitter Girls' favourite places to visit and they went there at least once every holiday. They'd first found out about the Donkey Sanctuary through Charly and Zoe's trips to the riding stables. One of the ladies who ran the stables had told them about the Sanctuary because she had adopted a donkey that was living there. The Sanctuary looked after donkeys that had no one else to care for them, or donkeys that were very old and needed somewhere peaceful to spend their days grazing.

The first time the Glitter Girls had visited the Sanctuary they had fallen completely in love with all the donkeys that lived there.

As soon as the donkey sanctuary was mentioned, the other Glitter Girls stopped their munching and bombarded Charly and Zoe with questions.

"What new donkeys?" Flo asked.

"Yes – when did they arrive there?" Meg wanted to know.

"Well," said Charly, pushing her pink glasses

back up her nose. "The donkeys have come from the seaside. They used to spend almost every day working on the beach."

"Doing what?" Meg wanted to know.

"They used to take children for rides up and down the beach," Zoe said.

"Ohhh!" Hannah said. She thought back to last year when she had gone on holiday with her mum, dad and brother to Spain. She and Joe had gone the whole length of the beach riding on donkeys. They even had a photograph of them doing it in the downstairs loo at home!

"So, what are their names?" Flo asked.

"That's the thing – no one knows!" Charly said. "It's really sad. . ."

"What do you mean, no one knows?" Hannah looked up indignantly. "Surely the person who looked after them at the beach must know their names!"

"Yes!" said Flo, twiddling her hair. "But that's what's so sad!" Zoe said. "The man who owned the donkeys died, and no one else can remember what he called them."

"Oh no!" said Hannah, who hated hearing sad stories. "But didn't he have any family? Surely *they* know what the donkeys are called?"

"I don't think he did," Charly said. "After the man died, no one knew what to do with the donkeys. So the local authority down at the beach asked the Donkey Sanctuary if they'd take them."

"And that's how they came to be there," said Zoe.

"Well, we've got to go and see them, haven't we?" Meg begged her friends.

"Yes, we have!" Hannah agreed.

"It's Saturday tomorrow," said Flo. "Why don't we go then?"

"Good idea!" Charly said.

the donkeys died and no one else can remember what he called them."

"Oh well," said Hannah, who hated boring sad stories. "But didn't he have any family? Surely they know what the donkeys are called?"

"I don't think he did," Charly said. "After the man died, no one knew what to do with the donkeys. So the local authority down at the beach asked the Donkey Sanctuary if they'd take them."

"And that's how they came to be there," said Zoe.

"Well, we've got to go and see them, haven't we?" Meg rubbed her hands.

"Yes, we have!" Hannah agreed.

"It's Saturday tomorrow," said Flo. "Why don't we go then?"

"Good idea!" Charly said.